THE RABBIT'S BRIDE

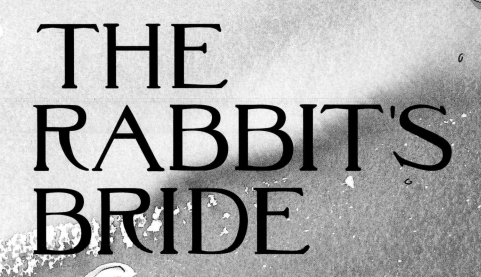

by the BROTHERS GRIMM

with pictures by HOLLY MEADE

Marshall Cavendish • New York

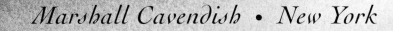

There was once a woman who lived with

her daughter in a beautiful cabbage garden.

And there came a rabbit who ate up all the cabbages.

At last the woman said to her daughter,
"Go into the garden, and drive out the rabbit."

"Shoo! Shoo!" said the maiden:
"don't eat up all our cabbages, little rabbit!"
"Come maiden," said the rabbit, "sit on my tail
and go with me to my rabbit hutch."

But the maiden would not.

Another time, back came the rabbit, and ate away
at the cabbages until the woman said to her daughter,
"Go into the garden, and drive away the rabbit."

"Shoo! Shoo" said the maiden.
"Don't eat up all our cabbages, little rabbit!"

"Come, maiden," said the rabbit, "sit on
my tail and go with me to my rabbit hutch."

But the maiden would not.

Again, a third time back came the rabbit,
and ate away at the cabbages until the woman said
to her daughter, "Go into the garden, and drive
away the rabbit."

"Shoo! Shoo!" said the maiden.
"Don't eat up all the cabbages, little rabbit!"

"Come, maiden," said the rabbit, "sit on my
tail and go with me to my rabbit hutch."

And then the girl seated herself on the rabbit's tail, and the rabbit took her to his hutch.

"Now," said he, "set to work and cook some bran
and cabbage. I am going to bid the wedding guests."

And soon they were all collected.
Would you like to know who they were?

Well, I can only tell you what was told to me.
All the hares came, and the crow who was to be the
parson to marry them, and the fox for the clerk,
and the altar was under the rainbow.

But the maiden was sad because she was so lonely.

"Get up! Get up!" said the rabbit.
"The wedding folk are all merry."

But the bride wept and said nothing, and the rabbit went away but very soon came back.

"Get up! Get up!" said he. "The wedding folk are waiting."

But the bride said nothing, and the rabbit went away.

Then she made a figure of straw and dressed it
in her own clothes and gave it a red mouth
and set it to watch the kettle of bran.

And then she went home to her mother.

Back again came the rabbit, saying "Get up! Get up!" and he went up and hit the straw figure on the head so that it tumbled down.

His bride did not get up because she was made of straw.

The wedding folk went home.

And the rabbit went away and was very sad.

Back in the beautiful cabbage garden,
the maiden's mother was happy.
And so was the maiden.

Dedicated to all the maidens
who take a ride with the rabbit.
And who with courage and
creativity find a way home. —H.M.

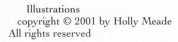

Illustrations
copyright © 2001 by Holly Meade

Marshall Cavendish, 99 White Plains Road, Tarrytown, NY 10591

Library of Congress Cataloging-in-Publication Data
Meade, Holly (date)
    The rabbit's bride / by the Brothers Grimm; [retold and] with pictures by Holly Meade
    p. cm.
    Summary: A retelling of the traditional tale in which a rabbit attempts to marry a young girl.
    ISBN 0-7614-5081-5
    [1. Fairy tales. 2. Folklore—Germany. 3. Rabbits—Folklore.] I.Grimm, Wilhelm, 1786-1859.
    II. Grimm, Jacob, 1785-1863. III.Title.
    PZ8.M465 Rab 2001   398.2'0452932—dc21   [E]   00-057013

The text of this book is set in point Cochin.
The illustrations are rendered in watercolor.

Printed in Hong Kong
First Edition

6 5 4 3 2 1

This version of *The Rabbit's Bride* by the Brothers Grimm
was translated from the German by Lucy Crane, and first
published in 1886.
That particular version ended the story with:
". . . he went up and hit the straw figure on the head, so
that it tumbled down. And the rabbit thought that he had
killed his bride, and he went away and was very sad.

The closing lines in this book differ because of changes made by Holly Meade